Marjory Past
Lamont
Sunday School
1953

The Triplets Take Over

by
BERTHA B. MOORE

WM. B. EERDMANS PUBLISHING COMPANY
Grand Rapids   1953   Michigan

Copyright, 1953, by
Wm. B. Eerdmans Publishing Co.

All rights in this book are reserved. No part may be reproduced in any manner without permission in writing from the publisher, except brief quotations used in connection with a review in a magazine or newspaper.

Set up and printed, April, 1953

PRINTED IN THE UNITED STATES OF AMERICA

WITH LOVE TO
PATRICIA JONES
AND
JIMMY CAIN

CONTENTS

1. The Triplets Listen to a Letter 7
2. The Triplets Say Goodbye to Their Father 17
3. The Triplets Take Over 27
4. The Triplets Receive Company 37
5. The Triplets Search for Rosebud 46
6. The Triplets Entertain Company 56
7. The Triplets Are Separated 69
8. The Triplets Have a Surprise 79

1

The Triplets Listen to a Letter

"MOM, come on out on the porch where it's cool to read your letter," Iva suggested when she carried the mail into the house to Mrs. Baer. "We'll all want to hear what Aunt Nell has to say."

"All right! I'd like to take time for a bit of cooling off," Mrs. Baer replied. "But be careful not to wake up Bobby."

The Baer triplets hurried to the porch where Ted held the screen door open for his mother and sisters. Then he sat on the porch floor where he could lean against a post. In the glider Iona sat on her mother's right while Iva took her left. Eagerly they watched as the envelope was opened and the letter removed. Aunt Nell, Mrs. Baer's youngest sister, was the triplets' favorite aunt.

"Well!" Mrs. Baer exclaimed, having read a few lines, all to herself.

"Oh, Mom, what does she say?" Iva coaxed.

"Please don't read it all to yourself first!" Iona added.

"Can't you girls wait a little minute?" Ted demanded, though he was just as anxious to hear the letter.

"Your Aunt Nell is in the hospital and your Uncle Ben wants your mother to come on the next train, or plane. He says to bring Bobby, but to leave you triplets at home!" she explained.

"Well, I like that!" Ted mumbled.

"Oh, is Aunt Nell very sick, Mom?" Iona asked, anxiously.

"Did she have an operation?" Iva wanted to know.

"Uncle Ben doesn't explain a thing! Ted, when you grow up, do remember to tell all you are supposed to tell when you write a letter as important as this one is," Mrs. Baer instructed her son.

"I'll try to remember," Ted promised.

"Mom, are you going?" Iva asked, not very enthusiastically.

"Are you, Mom? When? How?" Iona added, moving slightly nearer her mother in the porch glider.

"Unless your father thinks I had better stay here, I'll start on the first train I can catch after he comes home. I'm sure he will say for me to go. And that means some stepping around for all the Baers. Come on. Let's get busy!" And Mrs. Baer was

THE TRIPLETS LISTEN TO A LETTER 9

out of that glider while Iona and Iva decided they had better get busy, too. Ted jumped up so nimbly that he was ready to open the screen door for his mother.

"Mom, how long will you be gone?" Iona asked, as they entered the house.

"And who is going to take care of us?" Iva asked.

"I guess we're big enough to take care of our own selves," Ted reminded his sisters.

"Oh, well, Rosebud will be here to take care of us all," Iona remembered. "We'll get along just fine, Mom. Don't you worry the least little bit."

"I should say not!" quickly Iva agreed.

Ted grinned. "You knew all the time we could get along all right, didn't you, Mom?" he asked.

"I was perfectly willing to let you try it," she agreed, as she led the way to the kitchen. "Let's prepare Rosebud for what is likely to happen."

They heard Rosebud humming, "In the Sweet Bye-and-Bye." Mrs. Baer smiled and nodded to her triplets as she went into the kitchen.

"Rosebud, I have a surprise for you, and I hope it's going to prove sweet," Mrs. Baer announced.

"Do tell, Mis' Baer, and what is that surprise you got?" Rosebud asked, looking at the four Baers before her.

"I have had a letter from my sister Nell's husband, asking me to come at once to be with my sister because she is in the hospital. Ben didn't explain a thing, so I do not know how long I shall have to be away, but don't you agree that I should go? You and Mr. Baer and the triplets can get along just fine. Can't you?" Mrs. Baer asked, trustfully.

"Get along? 'Course we can! Don't you have the least bit of worriment about us. The good Lord and Mr. Baer will make a good team to see that we do jes' like you'd have us do. Is there some packin' and fixin' you want me to do for you, Mis' Baer?" Rosebud asked, her big black eyes looking a bit troubled.

In a very few minutes every one had a task to perform and Bobby slept on through the confusion. When he finally awoke, he climbed off his bed, listened for voices, and then made his way to his mother's room. For a moment he stood in the door, watching his mother as she packed a bag full of things his big sisters were handing to her. That was what happened when someone was going away!

"Bobby go along!" he announced before anyone discovered his presence.

Ted reached him first, lifted him to his shoulder, and said, "Where are you going, Bobby?"

"On a trip!" he announced joyously.

"Who is going with you?" Iona asked.

"Mommy is," Bobby replied.

So there was no trouble at all from young Bobby. He was the happiest one of the Baer family.

When Mr. Baer came home, he agreed immediately that Mrs. Baer should go to her sister. He telephoned about the train and made reservations for Mrs. Baer. So in a very few hours, the Baer household was telling Mrs. Baer and Bobby goodbye. Bobby was just a bit disturbed because his father was not going along.

"Do take care of one another," Mother Baer urged as the train whistled at the railroad crossing.

"Just remember that He who is watching over you and Bobby and Aunt Nell and all the others is also watching over us. Leave us in His care and, well, come on back to us as soon as you can!" Mr. Baer replied, picking up Bobby so he could carry him into the train.

Ted was close at his heels with the suitcase. Of course, he would have to get aboard with that!

Mother Baer snatched quick kisses from Iona and Iva. The train slowed to a stop.

"You girls had better wait for us where you are," Daddy Baer advised. "And Ted," he started to say, but Ted was already inside with the suitcase.

Iona and Iva watched till they saw their mother waving to them from a window. Then Bobby waved. They were so interested that they were a little startled when Ted yelled right beside them, "Bye! Have a good time, but hurry home!"

That fast train never did tarry long in the station, so, too soon for the triplets, it was puffing its way towards Aunt Nell. With a bit of a sigh, Daddy Baer said, "Well, suppose we go to the springs for the night!"

For a moment the triplets looked at him with big question marks in their eyes. Then grinning, Ted said, "That'll be fine, Dad. There is no place like the Bed Springs for night time."

"I thought you really meant we were going some place," Iva said, but not fussy.

"Do you know what, Dad? I think a glass of milk with some ice cream in it, all whipped till it was thick, would settle our nerves and help us to sleep lots better when we go to the springs," Iona suggested.

"That's a good idea. Do we have some at home?" Daddy Baer teased.

"We have the milk, but we ate all the ice cream. I meant at the drug store when it can be whipped thick better," Iona explained.

That is the reason the triplets and their father were so late that night in settling down upon the springs. It may be the reason Rosebud found them all asleep the next morning.

THE TRIPLETS LISTEN TO A LETTER 13

A knocking on his door awoke Daddy Baer. It took him almost a minute to realize what had happened the night before. He called, "All right! Is that you, Rosebud?"

"It sho' am, Mister Baer! Is you takin' a vacation?" she asked.

"No, ma'm! I'll be right down. And Rosebud, please call these sleepy heads and tell them to come right down to breakfast," he added, opening his door and hurrying into the bathroom before one of the triplets beat him.

Iona and Iva arrived in the kitchen ahead of Ted.

"Tell us what to do, Rosebud," Iona said. "Mom told us we were to help you all we could."

"Do tell, Mis' Iona! That was real thoughtful of her. Well, you fix the grapefruit with that little sharp pointed knife and Iva, you fill up the sugar bowl," Rosebud directed.

In popped Ted. "Good morning, Rosebud! What do you want me to do beside eat?"

"Fetch in the milk, if you please," Rosebud told him, with a very special smile.

When he was gone, Iona asked, "Rosebud, why do you say please to Ted and not to Iva and me?"

Rosebud's broad smile displayed her very white teeth. "I reckon it's because he'll be a man some day and women folks most always has to spoil the men folks," she replied, with a deep chuckle.

"That's exactly what makes it hard on their wives, too! Their mothers and sisters and everyone spoil them while they grow up and when they get married they expect their wives to keep on spoiling them. I don't want Ted to be spoiled!" Iva decided.

Ted came in with three quart bottles of milk in his arms. Grinning and winking at Rosebud, he said, "You're too late, Sis. I'm done and spoiled!"

That's when Daddy Baer came upon the scene.

"You are what?" he asked.

"He says he is already spoiled, Daddy. Is he?" Iona asked, giggling.

Ted blushed. Rosebud began humming, "Heavenly Sunlight," as she broke the eggs into the hot pan. Mr. Baer looked at his son and then at that son's sisters who were so much alike it was difficult to tell which was Iona and which was Iva.

"I'd not be a bit surprised if all three of you aren't spoiled a little bit, or are likely to be by the time your mother comes back. Rosebud, you and I shall have to be very careful about petting these three Baers too much!" he concluded very seriously.

"That's a fact, Mister Baer!" she agreed.

"Suppose we spoil you, Daddy!" Ted suggested.

"Let's do!" Iona agreed quickly.

THE TRIPLETS LISTEN TO A LETTER 15

"It will suit me," Daddy Baer agreed. "But let's settle down now to our morning Bible reading and prayer. Can you join us now, Rosebud?"

Rosebud drew up her very own chair and opened her Bible to the morning passage.

"It's my turn to read," Ted announced, opening the Bible that was usually kept on a corner of the table. "It's from the fourth chapter of First John. 'Beloved, let us love one another: for love is born of God; and every one that loveth is born of God, and knoweth God. He that loveth not knoweth not God; for God is love. In this was manifested the love of God toward us, because that God sent His only begotten Son into the world, that we might live through Him.' Daddy, does that mean the kind of love we have for our parents and each other? Or does it mean that we are to love everybody so that we are willing and want to do all we can in order for them to hear about Jesus and His love?"

"I think it is the kind of love that is forgiving and kind and anxious to have the unsaved come to a full knowledge of the Lord Jesus. Isn't that what you think, Rosebud?" Mr. Baer asked, kindly.

"I sho' do! And if more folks had that kind of love, the old world would be in a lot better fix. And that's a fact!" Rosebud declared.

Daddy Baer led the morning prayer, remembering to ask the Lord to take care of the sick Aunt

Nell and Mother Baer and Bobby as well as those who were home. He also remembered to pray for those who were leaders and for the missionaries, especially for those in Cuba some of whom Daddy Baer and the triplets had met when they had flown to Cuba.

Daddy Baer was having such a good time with his breakfast that he must have forgotten he could not keep on staying at the table. Suddenly he exclaimed, "Look at that clock!"

Daddy Baer jumped up. So did the triplets. It took all three of them to rush him off to work.

"Hurry home, Daddy!" Iva called after him.

2

The Triplets Say Goodbye to Their Father

THAT first day fairly flew by. Rosebud decided it was a good time to do some house cleaning, so she put each one to work separately so there could be no time lost in playing at the job. By noon Ted was so hungry he was sure Rosebud had forgotten to call that lunch was ready. He went to the kitchen to find out.

"Rosebud, is that clock right?" he asked, for he had to have some kind of excuse for appearing before he had thoroughly cleaned his room.

"'Course it's right! I has to keep it right all the time so's I'll not miss my radio programs. I reckon it was your stummick that got empty too fast so it made you think it was time to eat. Go call your sisters and you all can help set out your snack," she replied.

Ted dashed into the hall and yelled up the stairway, "Hey, you girls! Your snack is ready. Come and get it!"

They, too, must have been expecting a call, for immediately they came running.

It was a snack. Leftovers from two whole days back. But Rosebud had dressed them up with a squeeze of lemon juice, or a bit of extra seasoning or sugar. No one seemed to mind at all.

"I decided you all could plan dinner for your father. Each one may name one thing to have, but don't all three name a dessert," Rosebud suggested when all the leftovers had disappeared.

"Let's have a Mexican dinner," Iona suggested. "You know, all hot stuff."

"Oh, no! Not when the weather is so hot! I'd rather have an Eskimo dinner," Iva objected.

"An Eskimo dinner would be hotter than a Mexican dinner because it would be greasy. They eat lots and lots of fat, you know," Iona reminded her.

"Rosebud, I'll tell you what. Let's just have some of your good tamale pie. Dad likes that. So do we, and it's enough like a real Mexican dinner to do very well," Ted decided.

"Oh, that will be —" Iona began, but she did not finish, for Mr. Baer himself appeared in the door.

"Why, Daddy!" Iva exclaimed, pushing back her chair.

"We've eaten up all the scraps, Dad. Is that what you came home for at this time of day, some of our scraps?" Ted asked.

THE TRIPLETS SAY GOODBYE

Mr. Baer sat down at the table and asked for a cup of coffee. "I came home to break some more news," he said, sipping his coffee.

"Good news, or bad news, Daddy?" Iva asked.

"I hope it will be good. It all depends," he replied.

"What does it depend on?" Iona asked.

Mr. Baer gave a good look at each of the triplets. Then leaning back, he looked at Rosebud.

"Rosebud, coud you come and stay here at night?" he asked.

"Why, yes, suh! I reckon as how I could, Mista Baer. But how come you want to know that?"

"My boss wants me to go out of town for three, maybe four, days. I don't see how I can get out of going. But if I know you are here with these three Baers, day and night, too, I will feel free to go pack up a few things and make the trip. How about it?" he asked all of them.

"Of course, you should go, Daddy! We'll get along just fine," Iona assured him.

"I'll stay right here, Mista Baer, and won't let ary one of these chilluns out of my sight. And that's a fact," Rosebud declared.

"Will the three of you agree to mind Rosebud and do what you know is right and what your mother would want you to do if she were at home?" he asked the children.

"We promise, Dad. We'll do just what Mom would want us to do and just what we know the Lord Jesus wants us to do. If we do that, we'll be all right. Won't we?" Ted asked.

"No father could ask for more than that," Mr. Baer replied. "I wish you girls would help me find some clean shirts and the things I'll need to take along. Your mother always does things like that so I hardly know what to take. Will you know?"

"We'll do your packing," Iona and Iva exclaimed together, losing no time in jumping up to start upstairs.

"Ted, would you take another suit, or depend upon the one I wear?"

Ted studied a minute. Then he said, "I believe I'd take an extra suit, Dad. Something might get spilled on that one."

It took Rosebud, too, before the packing was all done and Mr. Baer stood in the front hall, waiting for a taxi. He was going to fly to the city where he was going.

"Dad, what will you do if your plane begins diving towards the ground?" Iona asked.

"If I am aware of what is happening, I hope the first thing I shall do is pray. Then if we aren't told to prepare to jump, I shall fasten my belt and brace myself for the crash, praying that somehow the good Lord will help the pilot to land safely," he explained.

"We'll be praying that nothing like that will happen, Daddy," Iva assured him.

"Let's bow our heads right now and commit us all and your mother and Bobby anew into our Lord's loving care," Daddy Baer suggested.

When the taxi arrived, Ted grabbed the suitcase and the girls grabbed their father's hands. Rosebud stood on the front steps and watched the procession go to the sidewalk.

"I got a feelin' somethin's goin' to happen, and that's a fact," Rosebud murmured. "O Lord, if somethin's got to happen, do please let it happen to me and not to ary one of these precious lambs what's in my care. Amen!" Then as Mr. Baer turned to wave to her, she waved, and called, "Goodbye. Come back safe!"

The taxi rolled down the street. The triplets stood still and watched it disappear. Then slowly for them, they started up the walk towards the house.

"Seems funny to be without a mother or a father at home," Iona said wistfully.

"I wonder which one will come home first," Iva added.

"I hope Rosebud doesn't keep us cleaning house the whole time," Ted remarked.

"Yes, and so do I!" agreed both sisters.

When they went inside they looked for Rosebud and of course, they found her in the kitchen.

"Now what are we going to have for dinner?" Ted asked.

"Rosebud, I've about finished my cleaning up. If I hurry, may I bake a chocolate cake?" Iva asked.

"Oh, and may I fix some ice cream for Ted to freeze in the real freezer? Would you, Ted?" Iona added, hopefully.

"Will you all clean up the messes you make?" Rosebud asked.

It certainly did not take long to finish the cleaning each had been assigned to do. Then Rosebud left the kitchen to them while she went home to prepare to return to spend the nights until one of the parents returned.

Ted finally consented to tie an apron around his waist. His objection had been, "Suppose someone comes!" His sisters assured him no one would come. Then they began. By the time Iva had her cake mixed and in the pans and Iona had her custard ready to heat and Ted had the ice cream freezer ready for the ice cubes and the salt, the kitchen looked a little as if a cyclone had struck it. But it did not matter. Before Rosebud had time to

THE TRIPLETS SAY GOODBYE 23

come back, they expected to have all the mess cleaned up.

The door bell rang!

"You go, Ted!" Iona said. "I have to stir this custard so it won't scorch. It has to come off at just the right minute!"

"I'll say me go! With this apron around my middle?" Ted exploded.

"Please go, Ted! I can't leave my cake," Iva pleaded.

Off came the apron with one quick jerk.

"If it's a stranger, shall I let him in?" Ted called as he went through the hall.

"No, sir!" both girls yelled.

"Maybe we should have gone, too," Iona said.

Then they heard voices. Ted had let someone in! Whoever it was, was coming right to the kitchen!

"If anything happens, you make a dash out that back door and yell for help!" Iva instructed Iona, who was nearer the back screen door.

"All right," Iona began to answer when Ted and his companion appeared.

"It's Sam!" both girls squealed.

"Hi!" was Sam's greeting.

"We thought you were somebody," Iva stammered.

"Well, I like that. I am somebody and whatever you're cooking smells mighty good," Sam told her.

"We're going to have ice cream and chocolate cake. Our mother never likes for her cakes to be cut while they are hot, but maybe this will be a little bit cool by the time you and Ted have the ice cream frozen. Did Ted tell you our parents are not home?" Iona asked.

"He began telling me something but never did finish. I guess it feels queer to you when your parents go off and leave you. I'm so used to being left all alone that I don't pay any attention to it anymore. I used to get so lonesome that I'd go to an early movie and stay through two showings of it. But I don't go much at all anymore since we went to camp and I learned to like to read my Bible and good books. Do you know what? I've read the Gospels through once and am starting over again. Sometimes my mother and father let me read a little bit to them. And do you know what else? They both liked your mother and father when they came to see us. I wish they'd come back and not wait for my parents to come to see them," Sam said, sitting at the window where he could be cool and watch this cooking business also.

"Maybe when they both come home again, they'll go and invite your parents to go with them to church," Ted said.

"That'd be fine. Say, is that the way you fix ice to make ice cream? My mother makes hers in the refrigerator," Sam announced.

"So does our mother most of the time, but it's lots better when it's made in a freezer. You just wait and see if it isn't," Iva said.

"Do you mean that I could stay and help eat some of your cake and ice cream?" Sam wanted to know.

"Of course, we do! We're glad you came," Ted assured him.

So when Rosebud came, she found an extra boy with a heaping saucer of ice cream and a big piece of chocolate cake, having a wonderful time with the triplets. She also found a messy kitchen!

"Looks like I'd better go back," she told them, as she stood with her hands on her broad hips. "I sho' come back too soon!"

"Oh, no, Rosebud! You are just in time. We're going to clean up every bit of our mess just as soon as we finish eating our ice cream. It will melt if we quit now. Here, Rosebud, I'll get you some. It's extra good!" Iva assured her.

Of course, Rosebud pronounced the cake delicious and the ice cream just about the best she had ever eaten. And of course, she helped a little bit with the mess. When it was about done, the telephone rang.

"Go ahead, Ted," Iona suggested.

Ted hurried to the telephone. When he returned, his face was beaming.

"You can't guess who it was!" he announced.

"It was Mom!" Iva squealed. "I can tell by the way you look."

"Yep! And she's okay and Aunt Nell is getting along all right. Mom said she'd not be home for three more days. I didn't tell her Dad is gone. She might have worried. So now when we hear from Dad, everything will be just right," Ted said.

"It's just right as 'tis. The good Lord's watchin' over your father," Rosebud reminded them.

3

The Triplets Take Over

"DO you suppose we ought to get up and help Rosebud with our breakfast?" Iona asked Iva, sleepily.

"Have you heard anyone stirring around yet? Have you heard her singing?" Iva yawningly asked in reply.

"No, but she must surely be up. It's almost eight o'clock. Let's get up and beat Ted downstairs," Iona suggested, sliding from the bed as she spoke.

But Ted played a trick on them. As they reached the foot of the stairs, he jumped out at them and both girls squealed.

"We'll get you for that, Ted Baer. See if we don't," Iona threatened.

Ted ran towards the kitchen, the girls at his heels. But he stopped short at the door.

"Rosebud!" Ted exclaimed. "What has happened?"

Rosebud groaned.

Rosebud was sitting on the floor right in front of the electric stove.

"I can't move, and that's a fact!" she exclaimed.

Iona and Iva knelt beside her. "Rosebud, what's wrong? Did you fall down?" Iona asked, anxiously.

"It's one of my old ketches in my old back. Maybe if Ted'd sorta get hold of me under my arms and you girls'd hold my hands and help pull me up, I could get back on my feet," Rosebud directed.

"You poor dear! Have you been sitting here long?" Iva asked, as the three tried to lift her almost two hundred pounds off the floor.

"Not long," Rosebud replied, groaning and doing all she could to rise. Drops of sweat fell from her chin. She bit her lips to keep back her cries of pain. It looked for a moment as if they could not make it, but they did. Rosebud swayed a little as Ted grabbed a chair and helped to ease her into it.

Rosebud looked up at the triplets and smiled. "Praise the good Lord, we made it!" she said.

"What can we do to help, Rosebud?" Iona asked.

"Do you want us to call the doctor?" Ted wanted to know.

Rosebud shook her head. "Don't call ary doctor. Jes' let me be here in the chair for a spell. Iona, honey, take that bacon off the stove and Iva, honey, look at the toast. Ted, would you please pour a cup of coffee for me?"

Like a commanding officer Rosebud sat and directed her troops. They made a sort of game of breakfast and then washing the dishes and putting the kitchen in order.

"Now what?" Ted asked, when there seemed to be nothing else to do.

"I've been a-thinkin'," Rosebud replied. "Like as not my old back won't get over this ketch 'fore your mother gets home. Supposin' a burglar'd try to get in. What good would I be? Supposin' the house'd get on fire. Like as not I couldn't move fast nuff to get out of the way. I'm jes' not ary bit of good and that's a fact."

"Oh, yes; you are!" Iona assured her. "Nothing's going to happen like a burglar and a fire. Aren't we asking God to take care of us?"

"Why don't you lie down and rest all day?" Iva wanted to know. "We'll go to the store and get lunch and dinner and take care of everything."

"How'd I ever get up if I'd get flat on my back? Looks like I'd better go home and send Pansy to take care of you chillun," Rosebud said with a great sigh.

"We don't need anyone to take care of us!" Ted declared. "We are not babies. If Pansy'd come here, who'd take care of you? Looks to me as if you need to stay here where we can wait on you. Don't you girls think so?"

"I do!" Iona announced.

"So do I! I'll tell you what. Let's see if you can get to the big chair by the window in the dining room. We'll lift your feet to the footstool and it would be almost like going to bed. Do you want to try it, Rosebud? We'd lots rather have you here with us and you not be able to do much but tell us what to do than to have Pansy."

It was not an easy move, but slowly inch by painful inch it was made. Ted brought in the morning paper. Iona put an end table beside the comfortable chair and laid the Bible upon it.

"We'll go make the beds now," Iva said, when it looked as if they could do no more.

"Do you want anything else, Rosebud?" Iona asked.

"Nary a thing. I feel like a regular queen, bein' waited on like this," Rosebud replied, smiling broadly.

Up the stairs raced the triplets. Iona pulled Ted into their room and closed the door.

"I think we ought to call Dr. Jim and tell him what's happened. We can't let poor Rosebud get stiffer and stiffer. She can't sleep in that chair all night!" Iona announced.

"She'll hear us," Ted reminded her.

"We could call from the extension in Mom's room and close the door," Iva suggested.

"Ted, you're the man of the house. You go call him," Iona said.

"I will if one of you will go make my bed, too. Rosebud will be expecting to hear me up over her," Ted agreed.

"I'll make it," Iva promised.

"What'll I tell him?" Ted asked, hesitating before he reached the door.

The girls exchanged glances. Then Iona said, "Tell him how she hurts and ask if he doesn't think he ought to come to see her."

Ted departed. Iva went to his room while Iona made the girls' bed. By the time Ted returned both rooms were in good order.

"What'd he say?" Iva demanded before Ted had time to explain.

"He's coming right away," Ted said. "Rosebud will fix us when she's able for calling a doctor for her."

"Maybe she will be glad," Iona hoped.

They lingered a bit longer and then decided they should go downstairs. "I'll sweep the front porch," Ted offered.

The girls tried to find something to do in the living room. So it was that Ted admitted the doctor and the girls met him as he entered the house.

"Good morning, young ladies! What have you done with my patient?" Dr. Jim asked, in his hearty, big voice.

"She's in here," Iva said, leading the way.

Rosebud was watching the door when her guests entered.

"Why, Dr. Jim! How come you stoppin' in here at jes' the time when we need you the mostest?" she asked, her face beaming in spite of her painful back.

"What's wrong, Rosebud? I know! You're too heavy on your feet!" he told her, removing his coat.

"It's not my feet, Dr. Jim. It's my ol' back, and that's a fact," Rosebud corrected him.

Dr. Jim took a good look at Rosebud. Then he cleared his throat and very earnestly said, "Lumbago!"

The triplets exchanged anxious glances.

"Is that very bad, Dr. Jim?" Ted asked.

Before he could reply, Iona added, "Is it catching?"

"Dr. Jim, don't send me to ary hospital," Rosebud pleaded.

Dr. Jim stretched out in his chair, threw back his head, and laughed. "Well, Ted, if you had it, you'd think it was bad. It's not catching, Iona. And Rosebud, we'll just play that you are already

THE TRIPLETS TAKE OVER

in a hospital and Ted is the intern and the girls are nurses. The quickest way to relief will be to tape this patient's back. So you girls fix her bed while Ted and I help her to her room."

When Dr. Jim left the Baer home, Rosebud was wearing a lot of adhesive tape on her back and she was instructed to lie as quietly as she could until after breakfast the following morning. She was to have her meals served as if she really were in a hospital.

Ted followed Dr. Jim to the door while the girls went to the kitchen for a drink for their patient, as well as for themselves. "How much is your bill, Dr. Jim?" Ted asked, rather anxiously, for he wondered how he could pay much of a bill and have enough left for their needs.

"Well, let me think. I'll tell you what. Suppose I send you a bill some day. If I happen to forget it, you don't need to remind me of it. Just let me forget it, and that's a fact, Ted!" he said, patting him on his shoulders.

So Ted's heart was much lighter when he went to his sisters. "How much did Dr. Jim charge, Ted?" Rosebud wanted to know at once.

Laughing, Ted replied, "He said he'd send a bill and if he forgot to not to remind him. Do you know what? I don't think he's going to charge us a red cent!"

"He's a plumb nice doctor, and that's a fact," Rosebud decided. "Can you chillun take care of yourselves if I take me a nap?"

"Of course, we can! We'll prepare our lunch. Is there anything special you'd like to have?" Iona asked.

"Sakes alive! The idea of me bein' asked what I'd like to eat! Anything, honey, jes' anything! What would your mother and father think if they could see me piled up in bed like this and you all waitin' on me jes' like I was somebody!" Rosebud replied, smiling as if she enjoyed being waited upon.

"But you are somebody! Look how you've taken care of all of us about ever since we can remember," Iva reminded her.

"We'll wake you up so you can eat your lunch," Ted told her.

As the triplets started down the hall, the telephone rang. "One of you answer it this time," Ted suggested.

Iona was nearest. As soon as she had spoken and had listened a moment, she put her hand over the transmitter, turned to Iva and Ted, and whispered excitedly, "It's long distance!"

"It's Dad!" Ted guessed.

"If it's Mom don't tell her about Rosebud and Dad," Iona said.

"O Daddy! Hello! Yes, sir; we're just fine. No, sir; she hasn't come home yet. Did you land topside up?" Iona asked, giggling.

"Ask him when he is coming home," Ted said.

"When are you coming home, Dad?" Iona asked. Then, "Not till then! Oh, yes; we'll get along just fine. No, sir! We haven't fussed a bit. Yes, sir! We remembered to pray for you and for Mom this morning, too. All right! Good-bye!"

"What'd he say?" Ted and Iva asked together.

"He won't be home before next week and he said for us to mind Rosebud. Well, I'm glad he called. Now we know that our parents are both all right," Iona said, sighing.

"Oh, there's the mail! I'll get it. I'll bring it to the kitchen," Iva said, running towards the front door.

"Don't you dare stop and read it before you bring it in," Ted called to her.

Perhaps she did not hear him. There were two letters. One she knew was from her mother because there was the return address in its corner. But the other one had no return address and the handwriting was brand new to Iva. She simply had to see who had sent it. So she took time to open the envelope. It was such a short letter that she read it in a jiffy. Then she rushed into the house, forgetting not to slam the screen door. Ted and Iona were waiting in the kitchen.

"You look all excited," Iona told her.

"Yes; and she opened one of the letters," Ted added. "Who's it from. You do look excited. What'd it say?"

"You just wait till you've read it. You'll be plenty excited, too. It never rains but it pours, as Mom has said, and it's certainly pouring on us!" Iva replied.

"Well, go ahead and read the letter," Ted ordered.

"Read it for yourself. I want to see what Mom said," Iva told him, handing the letter to Ted, but Iona was the one who took it.

4

The Triplets Receive Company

"WELL, of all things!" Iona exclaimed, when she had read the letter.

"I'll say it is pouring!" Ted added.

"What shall we do about it?" Iva asked.

"Do? Can we do anything at all? They are practically here right this minute! Didn't you realize it is this very day they will arrive?" Ted asked, opening the letter again. "Here it is. 'We'll be there Tuesday afternoon and we'll stay a week.' This is Tuesday and it is almost afternoon."

"Didn't they say how they're coming? Do we have to meet them at the depot, or the bus station?" Iona wanted to know.

"There's not a single solitary word about how they are coming. Well, there's one good thing about it. We don't have to go meet them some place. But what'll we ever do with them for a week when Mom and Dad are gone and Rosebud has lumbago?" Ted demanded, looking very perplexed.

"We'll have to do the best we can. And we'd better be getting at it this minute. Let's get lunch in a jiffy and take Rosebud hers and then clean up the mess we've made," Iva suggested.

"What did Mom say?" Ted asked. "When is she coming home?"

"Oh, yes; what did she say? We got so flabbergasted with the other letter that we plumb forgot Mom's. How is Aunt Nell?" Iona added.

"Mom won't be home till Wednesday of next week! Aunt Nell is getting better and Bobby is fine. Now let's get to work," Iva explained.

When they were in the kitchen, Iona suggested, "Let's open a can of soup. It's the easiest and quickest thing to fix."

"Rosebud doesn't like soup," Iva reminded her.

"We can eat the soup with some sandwiches and crackers and Rosebud can have, well what?" came from Ted.

The girls looked in the refrigerator and in the food cupboard. "She likes baked beans and scrambled eggs," Iona suggested.

So while Rosebud ate baked beans and scrambled eggs and coffee the triplets ate soup and crackers and peanut butter sandwiches and drank milk.

"What shall we have tonight?" Iona asked, as she swallowed her last bite.

The doorbell rang!

The triplets looked at each other and Ted almost choked on his peanut butter sandwich.

THE TRIPLETS RECEIVE COMPANY   39

"Do you suppose they are here already?" Iona gasped.

"Ted, go see who it is, but remember to find out before you unlatch the screen door," Iva said.

"You girls come along. I'm not going to meet them by myself," Ted objected.

The triplets started rather slowly to the door while the bell kept ringing. Whoever was ringing it stood at one side where he could not be seen. But the triplets did see a taxicab starting to leave in front of their house.

As they reached the door, a young bandit, not as tall as Ted, but dressed in full cowboy regalia with a black handkerchief hiding the lower part of his face and two toy pistols in his hands, stepped into view. Behind him was a girl, dressed as a cowgirl, who was perhaps a year older. She was trying to look fierce, but it was hard work for her merry blue eyes.

"This is a holdup! Let us in and turn over all your money and valuable jewelry to us. And don't yell or try to call the police," the young bandit ordered.

Ted held his hand on the screen door latch. Iona and Iva stood beside him.

"What do you think you are, Wayne Maynard? Take that ugly black handkerchief off your face and put those crazy pistols in your belt and quit acting silly. Then we'll let you in," Ted announced.

"Aw, can't you take a joke?" Wayne whined. But he put his pistols away and uncovered his face. "I wasn't actually trying to hold you up!"

"We don't even like to play that way," Ted told him, opening the door. "Come on in. Come in, Diann."

The company had come, cousins of the triplets from the country. They had never visited in a big city before, so were expecting to have a wonderful time.

The girls took Diann to their room while Ted took Wayne to his. And when they all came downstairs again, the visitors were wearing much cooler clothes. They looked just like normal, ordinary children.

"Wayne, Iona and Iva don't have any cowgirl suits," Diann informed her brother.

"I know. Neither does Ted. And we supposed all the boys and girls in the city wore them. But I'm glad they don't. They are awful hot!" Wayne admitted.

"I just don't see any fun in pretending to be a bandit or a thief or a robber. I don't expect to be one when I'm a man. It's all wicked and wrong," Ted explained.

"Oh, I'm not going to be a robber when I'm a man either. But there isn't any harm in playing like it now," Wayne defended himself.

"Yes there is! You could learn a lot of tricks by playing robber. Then when you grow up, you might want to try the very same tricks on people. I'd hate to spend a part of my life in prison. Wouldn't you?" Ted asked.

"Who said I was going to? I told you I was just playing a joke on you," Wayne repeated.

"Cowboys usually aren't robbers. Real cowboys work with cattle on big ranches. We saw lots of them when we drove home from California. I'd like to live on a big ranch and ride a pony," Iva said.

"I ride our big horse. It's fun," Diann told them.

"Do you wear your cowgirl suit?" Iona wanted to know.

Diann turned up her short nose. "I should say not! When I'm doing real farm work, I wear overalls just like Wayne and a big straw hat. Usually I go barefooted too. I don't suppose anyone actually wears all this rigging except in picture shows or rodeos. Do you go to picture shows just about every night?"

The triplets exchanged glances. Did they?

"If all the city boys and girls went to as many picture shows as we do, they'd certainly not see many," Ted told her.

Then Wayne and Diann exchanged glances. They were disappointed glances.

"We'd better go see about Rosebud," Iona remembered.

"She'll be wondering who's here," Iva added. "Come on, Diann. She'll want to see you and Wayne."

"Who is Rosebud?" Diann asked.

"You'll find out," Ted told her.

When they reached Rosebud's room, Ted and his sisters stepped aside for Diann and Wayne to go in first. And what they saw certainly surprised them. Upon her white bed lay Rosebud, her dark brown face looking darker against the white pillow. She looked even larger than she really was.

"Hello! And who are you?" Rosebud asked.

"We're Wayne and Diann Maynard," Diann stammered.

"They are our cousins from the country, Rosebud. They've come to visit us for a whole week," Iona informed her.

Rosebud gasped and just stared from one to another. "Do tell! Is that a fact? And me down with lumbago! Whatever will you poor lambs do?" Rosebud asked, sighing deeply.

"We aren't poor lambs! We are big Baers! And you'll be able to be up tomorrow if you stay in bed like a good girl today. Don't you worry a bit about us. We'll get along just fine," Iva assured her.

"Don't worry about us," Ted added.

"Rosebud, I guess we'll have to go to the grocery store. Hadn't we better go soon? Will you be all right while we're gone?" Iona asked.

"Of course, I'll be all right. Trot along, but don't buy the whole store out," Rosebud warned them.

"Would it be all right for us to have hot dogs for dinner?" Ted asked.

"If you'd not make a whole meal on just hot dogs," Rosebud agreed.

So all five youngsters started to the grocery store. Usually they rode their bicycles, but since their guests had none, they all walked. The neighborhood store was a large supermarket.

As they went in Wayne gave a surprised whistle. Diann said, "This is the biggest store I ever saw!"

Well, the triplets felt so important that they wished they could fill both trays of their carts. When the top tray was about filled, Iva said, "We'd better not get anything else until we see if we have money enough for what we already have."

"But we haven't any hot dogs yet," Ted remembered.

"Don't get but one package," Iva warned.

"Want to go with me, Wayne?" Ted invited.

The girls made their way to the cashier. By the time they were being checked the boys came with the frankfurters. They had some rolls also.

The bell of the cash register clanged. The cashier said, "Ten dollars and eighty-six cents!"

The triplets gasped.

"We haven't got but ten dollars!" Ted admitted.

"What can we take out that costs eighty-six cents?" Iva asked.

Smiling the cashier set aside a jar of salted nuts, a bag of stick candy, and a package of fancy cookies. Then the amount was nine dollars and ninety-seven cents!

Everything was put into four bags. Diann, being company, did not have to carry any. On the way home she said, "I didn't know it cost so much to eat in the city! Why, ten dollars doesn't buy much at all!"

"What'll we eat next week? Dad thought twenty dollars would be plenty to leave us," Ted said.

"I guess he didn't know you'd have two extra mouths to fill," Wayne said.

When they had set their groceries on the kitchen table, Iva said, "We'd better go tell Rosebud we are back."

THE TRIPLETS RECEIVE COMPANY

"You treat her like one of the family," Diann decided.

"Of course, we do! She's just like one of the family. She took care of us when we were babies," Iona told her.

They found Rosebud's bed empty, nicely made, and her room in order. But they did not find Rosebud!

5

The Triplets Search for Rosebud

TED, Iva, and Iona simply stood and looked at the empty bed, at the empty room.

"Well!" Ted exclaimed. "Dr. Jim must have made her well in a hurry."

"Has she been sick long?" Diann asked.

"Just since morning, but she could hardly move. She's got lumbago. Dr. Jim came and taped her back with a whole lot of adhesive tape. I wonder where she is," Iva explained.

"We'd better go put all this stuff away," Iona decided. "She'll be coming out in a minute, and will she tell us what's what when she sees what we've bought and finds out that we've already spent half of our allowance."

"We'd better go put those hot dogs into the refrigerator," Ted added.

So back to the kitchen they went, expecting to find Rosebud there. It took them fifteen minutes at least to find places for everything. There had to be some sampling done of the prunes and grapes, the cookies and sugar-coated cereal. But when the last bit of food was out of sight Rosebud had not made her appearance.

"Let's go see if she's back in her room," Iona suggested.

They ran down the hall to Rosebud's room, peeped in, and then walked in boldly. Rosebud had not returned.

"I'll look in the bathroom. Maybe she started to take a bath and couldn't get out of the tub!" Iva guessed.

They all watched Iva open the bathroom door slowly. No Rosebud was in the bathtub!

"But where can she be?" Iona asked, anxiously.

"I guess that's what we'd all like to know. Let's look outside. Maybe she went out and fell down," Ted suggested.

Out-of-doors the five trooped. They looked everywhere. She was not even in the garage. They came back in through the front door. She was not on the glider.

"Let's look in every room downstairs. Her back was too stiff for her to have gone upstairs and we'd hear her move around if she could have gone up there," Iva suggested, beginning with the living room. When they were ready to return to the kitchen they had found no Rosebud.

"I guess she was kidnapped," Wayne said. "That's what happens to people in my comic books.

Some mean persons come along and throw someone in a car and drive off and then hold them for a whole lot of money."

Even though they were really anxious about Rosebud, the triplets had to laugh a little. "I'd like to see anyone trying to throw our Rosebud into a car!" Ted said. "Maybe she went home. Let's call Pansy and ask her."

But Pansy said Rosebud was not there!

"How come you all want to know why she is home for?" Pansy asked.

"We went to the store and when we got back we couldn't find her anywhere so we thought maybe she'd gone home for something. Don't worry, Pansy. I guess she's just around here somewhere," Iona told her.

"Maybe she went to a neighbor's house to borrow something," Diann suggested.

"Iona, you and Diann go to the Smith's house. Iva, you go to the Current's. Wayne and I'll stay here and look in the basement," Ted directed.

In a few minutes they were all back in the kitchen. No one had found a trace of Rosebud. They all sat down around the table.

"I just don't see what has happened to her," Iona sighed. "If she didn't have lumbago, I'd not be so worried."

"Do you know what we haven't done?" Ted asked.

"No! What?" Iva asked.

"We haven't asked the Lord Jesus to help us find her," he replied.

"How could He help you find her? Does He know where she is?" Wayne asked.

"Of course, He does! He knows all about every single, solitary one of us," Ted told him.

"Would He hear you if you asked Him to help find her?" Diann asked.

"Of course, He would! He always hears us when we pray," Iona said.

"Would that be praying?" Wayne asked.

"Yes, it would! And we'd just better do that very thing. Let's get down on our knees so we'll really mean it. Iva, you ask Him to help us find Rosebud," Ted said.

Down upon their knees they knelt. Diann and Wayne watched a moment before they knelt, but soon all five were kneeling. Then Iva prayed, "Dear Jesus, we can't find Rosebud anywhere. We know that Thou couldst put Thy hand upon her right this minute because Thou dost know where she is. Please take care of her and bring her back. If she needs us, please help us to know where to go for her. We thank Thee for hearing our prayer. In Jesus' name. Amen."

As they arose, they heard what sounded like a sob from someone in the hall. Ted hurried out first.

"Rosebud!" the others heard him exclaim.

Then Rosebud was in the kitchen with her arms around the two girl Baers. Tears were glistening on her brown cheeks.

"Where were you, Rosebud?" Ted asked, a broad smile upon his face.

"I was up in your Mom's room, puttin' things away. Then I just sat down in her big chair and got to readin' her Bible. I heard you chilluns down here, but I didn't 'low you all could be lookin' for me. I had to come down the stairs slow like and didn't make a noise. I heard you all in the kitchen. But I didn't know there was a prayer meetin' goin' on. But bless my soul and body when I got where I could hear, I heard you precious lambs a prayin' about me! And that's a fact! So the good Lord was answerin' you all's prayers 'most 'fore they was prayed. And that's jes' like Him!" Rosebud declared, hugging Iva and Iona.

"Are you well now?" Ted asked.

"I'm a big sight better, Teddy. That Dr. Jim sho' knows how to fix up a lumbagoed back!" Rosebud replied.

"Rosebud, we got the frankfurters. And we spent all of the ten dollars but three cents!" Iona ventured to confess.

"Did you have a good time spendin' all that money?" Rosebud asked, chuckling away down deep in her throat.

"Yes, we did! But we didn't know it was going to be that much. We had to put some back because we'd picked out more than ten dollars' worth. But it was fun!" Iona replied.

"I'd never been in such a big store. I'd like to have a hundred dollars to buy everything I wanted," Diann said, giggling a bit.

"It would sho' take it," Rosebud said. "Well, we'll eat big for a day or two and then we'll do a lot of rememberin' and eat real plain."

"You'll have to help us make a list and we'll have to stick to it," Iva suggested.

What a delicious dinner they had that night! Wayne and Diann called it supper. They ate dinner at noon out in the country and supper for the evening meal. "That's the way they do down at Grandpa Baer's," Ted had said.

Ted and Iva prepared the hot dogs and by the time they were ready they were hot! Iona cut cabbage very fine for slaw to eat with the frankfurters. Wayne chopped the onions, but they were Bermuda onions so were not so tearful. When the frankfurters, slaw and onions, mustard and catsup were all inside one ordinary roll, it took a good, big mouth to get a full bite of it.

To serve with the frankfurters they had bought potato chips and tomato juice. For dessert there was blackberry pie topped with plenty of strawberry ice cream. Only Ted and Wayne were able to eat a second helping because every single one had eaten two frankfurters.

"This was the best supper I've had in a long, long time, since the preacher and his wife had supper at our house and our mother cooked almost all day Saturday and finished up Sunday morning. But it wasn't any better than this has been. The preacher asked the blessing just like Ted. Do you ask a blessing every time you eat, even when you don't have company?" Wayne asked.

"Of course, we do! Aren't you just as thankful for something to eat when you don't have company as when you do have?" Ted asked.

"Oh, yes; but we don't ask a blessing unless we have company that Mom knows would expect it. I guess we ought to do it all the time though," Wayne admitted.

"Do you have ice cream every day?" Diann asked, making the last bite of ice cream and pie last as long as possible.

"Maybe not every day, but nearly every day in the summer time," Iva replied.

"We don't have it except when Dad brings ice out from town and we make it in the ice cream freezer. That's just on special occasions, like the Fourth of July and birthdays and when special company comes," Wayne explained.

"We don't have electricity yet. We hope to before another year," Diann added.

The triplets looked at their cousins.

"Where do you get your water?" Ted asked.

"We have to draw it up out of a deep well," Wayne replied.

Rosebud chuckled the way she always did when she was amused. "That's how I growed up! We didn't have inside water. We had to tote ours from the spring. On Sat'day nights we got scrubbed in the wash tub, the least one first and the oldest one last. I was in betwixt so by the time my turn come, the water was already soapy. In the warm weather we went to the creek. That was fun."

"We go to the creek, too," Diann said.

"We'll have to visit you someday before you get electricity," Iona suggested.

So the first day ended. Rosebud had sat in a chair and "bossed" the dishwashing after dinner. Ted had swept the floor. Then everyone went into the living room to find out if they wanted to hear a radio program.

"Don't you have a television?" Wayne asked.

Ted shook his head. "We don't want one," he said.

"I don't see why! Then you could see what's going on. We thought you'd have a television and would go to picture shows and do lots of things you don't seem to be going to do," Wayne admitted.

"We might have television some day when the programs are better. I'd rather read a good book than go to a picture show unless it's an educational picture, especially one made in a real foreign country, or a good religious picture," Ted said.

They found some good musical programs, listened a while. Then Rosebud yawned. "Would you all 'cuse me, please? I'd better put my lumbago to bed."

"Let's have our family devotions and prayer before you go, Rosebud, just as we do when our parents are home," Ted suggested.

Ted read the Twenty-third Psalm, thinking his cousins would be more familiar with that than anything he could select. Then Iona led the prayer, remembering to pray for their cousins' family back home as well as their own father and mother and young brother and Aunt Nell and her family. "And we thank Thee for taking care of Rosebud today.

THE TRIPLETS SEARCH FOR ROSEBUD

We thank Thee because she is better. Bless her family, too, and bless boys and girls all over the world. Send missionaries to them to tell them how much Jesus loves them. Please keep us safe through the night. In Jesus' name we pray. Amen."

"It's almost nine o'clock. Let's all go to bed," Ted suggested.

"Do you know what we'd better do before we go to bed?" Iona asked.

"No. What?" her brother and sister asked.

"Ted, you'd better write Dad a letter and Iva and I'd better write one to Mom," Iona said.

"All right," Ted agreed. "Come on, Wayne. You can write to your Dad, too."

So all the Baers, including Rosebud, went to their rooms for the night. After all, the day had been rather exciting.

6

The Triplets Entertain Company

DIANN slept in Iva's bed and Iva slept with Iona. They were twin beds, but the girls were quite comfortable. Wayne slept in Bobby's bed in the room with Ted.

Iva awoke first on the second day the cousins were there. She lay awake for a few minutes, wishing Iona would waken so they could slip out, call Ted without disturbing Wayne, and go down and have a conference with Rosebud. Iva decided the family needed to do some planning about these visitors. But Iona slept on soundly just as if she had not slept all night long. Finally Iva gave her a slight punch. Iona stirred. Iva gave her another little punch. Iona opened her eyes.

"Wake up!" Iva whispered. "But don't make a sound. Let's get up and go down and talk to Rosebud before Diann and Wayne come down. Let's see if we can get Ted without waking Wayne."

"Why do you want to talk with Rosebud?" Iona whispered, yawning.

"I can't tell you here. Come on! You'll find out. It's important," Iva declared, getting up quietly.

"Oh, all right," Iona agreed, slipping from her side of the bed.

The sisters eased out into the hall with their clothes in their hands.

"I'll go see if I can get Ted up," Iva whispered.

Ted was lying on his back with his arms stretched out, sound asleep. Wayne was asleep also. Iva went to Ted's bedside and leaned close to his ear. "Ted! Ted! Wake up!" she whispered, pinching his ear a little.

Ted scratched his ear.

"Ted! Wake up!" Iva repeated.

Ted sat up in bed and looked at Iva. She put her hand over his mouth because he was about to speak out. "Don't wake up Wayne!" she warned. "Get your clothes and come on!"

Well, Ted certainly did not understand such goings on, but he did as he was told. In a very few minutes the Baer triplets were in the kitchen.

"What's this all about?" Ted wanted to know.

"It's just this. What are we going to do with and for Diann and Wayne? This is their first visit to a city. They came expecting to have a very exciting time going to movies, watching television, having stacks of comic books to look at, and no telling what else. And here we are with nothing to offer them. But we don't want to disappoint them too much. We can't say a word to each other when they get up because they'll be with us every minute. So let's do some planning now," Iva explained.

Rosebud made her appearance at that very moment. She was not as straight and erect as she usually was, but she was able to smile.

"Is breakfast ready?" she asked, giving her deep chuckle.

"You just sit down and we'll soon have it ready," Iona promised.

"You're just in time to help us do some planning," Iva began to explain. "Maybe you can tell us something to do that will help our cousins have a good time while they are here. Do you know some place we could go, or something we could do, Rosebud?"

Rosebud eased herself into a chair. She looked from one to another of her "precious lambs." "Your mother said you all need some new Sunday socks. Why don't you all take your cousins down to the big departmental store and ride on the elevator and the escalator? And I need a new paring knife from the ten cent store. How'd that do?"

"O Rosebud! You've saved the day! We can go downtown on the bus which will be something else new to them. Rosebud, could we go this

THE TRIPLETS ENTERTAIN COMPANY 59

morning and eat lunch at the cafeteria? Could we spend that much money?" Iona asked.

"I've still got this week's allowance and some of last week's," Ted ventured. "Have you girls spent all of yours?"

"Of course not! Oh, let's hurry and get breakfast and get everything all fixed up so Rosebud won't have to do a lot of stirring around and go right away. Tell us what to do for breakfast, Rosebud," Iva said, jumping up and looking ready to pitch into something.

"Why don't we just eat some of that new cereal we bought yesterday that's already sweetened and eat just plain bread without going to the trouble of toasting it, and well, some sliced bananas on the cereal?" Ted suggested.

"That won't take long at all! Ted, you run up and tell Wayne and Diann to come right down!" Iva said.

"I'll have to perk a cup of coffee, I reckon," Rosebud said, starting to rise.

"Just sit still, Rosebud. I'll fix your coffee," Iona offered.

Well, by half-past nine the Baer triplets and their country cousins were waiting at the corner for the bus. Rosebud watched from the front porch. They waved to her as the bus stopped. Then they were off.

Wayne and Diann sat next to windows. This city was a whole lot larger then they had ever dreamed it was!

"Could we go up in one of those great big high buildings?" Wayne asked Ted.

"We could take you up in the one Dad works in. We know the elevator man and he would let us go plumb to the top!" Ted replied.

Wayne's eyes opened wider. "Let's do that!" he exclaimed.

When they left the bus, Ted asked, "Where shall we go first?"

Without hesitation Wayne replied, "Let's go to the top of that high building you talked about."

"Okay! We'll go see where Dad works and ask Mr. Dick to take us to the very top floor," Ted said.

When they stood on the sidewalk before the building, it was difficult to see the top. Eagerly they went inside. No one else was waiting for the elevator.

"Well, look who's here!" Mr. Dick exclaimed. "I don't think I've seen your father today."

"He's out-of-town. These are our cousins, Wayne and Diann, Mr. Dick. They want to go to the very top of one of these high buildings. Would you please shoot us to the top of this one? Then we'll drop down to the sixth floor where Dad works," Ted explained.

THE TRIPLETS ENTERTAIN COMPANY 61

"Step right in, and face the front of the cage. Hold tight to your stomachs!" Mr. Dick said, slyly winking at Ted.

Diann got in between Iva and Iona and Wayne stood close to Ted. Mr. Dick closed the door. "Here we go!" he said. Well! No one squealed. They couldn't. It was the fastest ride Ted had ever had, much less his cousins. As the elevator reached the top floor it lost some of its speed and its occupants caught their breath again.

The elevator stopped. Mr. Dick opened the door. "How did you like that ride?" he asked, his eyes twinkling.

"Whee! That was a fast one!" Wayne cried, swallowing with a little difficulty.

"Go to the end of the hall and look out the windows," Mr. Dick said. "When you are ready to go down, ring for me. I'll come right up."

"I still feel funny," Diann said, as the group started down the hall. "I thought everything in the middle of me would come to the top of me."

"I felt as if my feet wouldn't stay on the floor!" Wayne giggled.

They looked down into the street from the window.

"Oh, it makes me dizzy!" Diann cried.

"People don't look much bigger than flies!" Wayne exclaimed. "And what little automobiles!"

They ran to the opposite end of the hall and looked from that side. Presently Iona said, "Let's go down. We don't want to spend too much time up here."

Wayne pressed the button that would bring Mr. Dick up after them. But it was not Mr. Dick. The door of the second elevator opened. It was Mr. Bruce.

"Well, bless my heart! Hello! What are you Baers doing away up here?" Mr. Bruce asked.

"We're showing the city to our cousins, Wayne and Diann," Iona told him. "Will you please take us down to the sixth floor so we can peep into the office where Dad works?"

"I'll do that very thing. Face the front, everybody!" And down they dropped.

"Are we there?" Diann asked, opening her eyes.

"Didn't you like that?" Mr. Bruce asked.

"It was fun, but it was scary, too!" Diann admitted.

The door to the outer offices was open. Ted stopped just as they reached it. "We can't go inside," he whispered. "But Dad works in one of the rooms off this big outer office. You can peep into this big office."

Wayne and Diann tiptoed till they could see into the big office. Ted ventured with them. Then they all tiptoed back.

"Your Dad must be awful important," Wayne decided.

"I guess he is," Ted admitted, proudly.

"Our Dad's important, too. I guess we need farmers to raise our food or the fathers in the cities couldn't work," Diann said, as she pressed the elevator signal.

It was Mr. Dick's elevator that came for them. "Don't go down so fast this time. Make it last longer," Wayne suggested.

"All right, sonny," Mr. Dick agreed. And the elevator went down much more slowly.

"Thanks! That was nice," Diann told him as they left the elevator.

"It wasn't so exciting though," Ted said.

They saw a big clock.

"I wish you'd look! It's eleven o'clock already. Let's go to the nearest ten cent store and then have our lunch," Ted suggested.

"Are we going to eat downtown?" Wayne asked.

"Yes, siree!" Iva exclaimed, taking Diann's hand.

"Now remember, we've got to all stay close together. And if anyone gets lost, hunt a policeman and tell him you want him to send you to Mr. Robert Baer's house. But no one will get lost if we stick together," Ted directed.

"I'll stay close to you, Ted," Wayne said.

"And we'll keep Diann with us," Iona added.

So into the huge ten cent store they went.

"How in the world will you ever find a paring knife in here?" Diann asked.

"We'll look around for a while and if we don't see any, we'll ask a clerk," Iva told her.

It was fun wandering around in the big store where it looked as if everything except ten cent things were displayed.

"How can they ever sell all these things?" Wayne asked.

Suddenly Diann exclaimed, "I see some knives! Is this the kind Rosebud wants?"

It was!

When it was safely in the purse Iona was carrying, Ted said, "I'm hungry! Let's find a cafeteria and eat!"

"That's what I say, Ted," Wayne agreed instantly.

The girls needed no persuasion.

"There's the one in the next block that Dad takes us to," Iva directed.

Presently they were lined up, awaiting their turn for trays, silver, napkins, and food. Ted led, Wayne was next, then, Iva, Diann, and Iona. Ted carried the money. They had been warned about filling their trays too full.

Everyone passed up the meats! The triplets each accepted an ear of yellow sweet corn. Not so the cousins. They had corn at home! They reached the salads. Ted selected two jello salads. So did Wayne. Iva selected one fruit jello and a salad of pickles and olives and celery. Diann had watched Wayne. She chose the jello salads. Ted took whole wheat rolls. So did everyone else. Ted selected lemon pie. Wayne took lemon pie and strawberry short cake. So did Diann. Ted took a tempting pudding. So did Wayne. And Diann. Ted said lemonade. Wayne said lemonade and iced tea.

They found a table for five. As they spread their dishes before them, Wayne asked, "Could we have some ice cream after while?"

"Sure! We'll get hungry before we go home," Ted agreed.

How good everything was! When his dishes were all empty, Wayne said, "I've still got some room!"

"Wayne Maynard! Haven't you any manners at all?" his sister asked. "Don't make a pig of yourself."

"Couldn't you eat any more?" Wayne asked her.

"Not till we have some ice cream in a little while," she replied.

"We'll go to the 'departmental' store now," Iona said, as they left the cafeteria where people were still standing in a long line.

"The what?" Diann asked.

"Rosebud calls it the departmental store. It's really a big department store. It has just lots of different departments in it," Iva explained.

"We're going to buy some Sunday socks," Iona told her.

What a big store! What a lot of people!

"Let's go up on the escalator first," Ted suggested.

"What's that?" Wayne asked.

"It's moving steps. You just step on the bottom one and it takes you up to the next floor," Ted explained.

They stood for a moment, watching people stepping upon the unfolding steps. "Do you want to try it now?" Ted asked.

"Sure! You go first and pull me on," Wayne said.

Ted held Wayne's hand. He did not have to hold it long. He was going up just like Ted, and Diann was going up just like Iona and Iva. The only trouble was the second floor was reached too soon. And how did a person get off? Ted stepped off. Wayne jumped. He bumped into a fat man, but he just smiled at him. Diann did a little better.

"Do you want to try some more?" Ted asked.

They went to every floor, finding all sorts of things. Wayne wanted to stay longer where the

THE TRIPLETS ENTERTAIN COMPANY 67

wagons and bicycles were. But the girls wanted to go on.

"Why don't you go ahead and buy the socks and let us boys look at the things we like to see," Ted suggested.

His sisters hesitated. Rosebud had said for them to be sure to stay together. But finally Iona said, "If you'll promise to keep Wayne right with you and meet us at the entrance in exactly half an hour so we can have our ice cream and go home, we'll go on."

"You can't find the socks and have them bought by that time. Give us an hour," Ted said. "It's almost two o'clock now. We'll be at the entrance at three. And you girls be sure to be there!"

Off went the girls. Back to the wagons and various sports goods went the boys. At five minutes till three the girls were ready to meet them in the entrance.

"I hope they won't keep us waiting long. I'm ready for my ice cream," Diann said.

"So are we," Iona admitted.

At three-fifteen the boys had not shown up. At three-thirty they had not arrived.

"What'll we do?" Diann asked, anxiously.

"Ted knows the way home," Iona said, slowly.

"Yes, but he promised to meet us here at three sharp. Maybe he missed us some way and went home. I've a notion to go on home, too," Iva said.

"Without any ice cream?" Diann asked.

"Rosebud will have some for us. Maybe we'd better go on home," Iona agreed. "But what'll we do if the boys aren't there?"

"We'll get the police to look for them," Diann suggested.

"Let's take one more good look and if we don't find them we'll go. You stay here and I'll see if I can find them," Iona said.

She returned alone. "Let's go on home," she said, almost in tears.

So home went the girls!

7

The Triplets Are Separated

"YOU just wait till I get hold of Wayne Maynard. I'll give him a piece of my mind!" Diann declared. "He knew better than to want to stay there with those old wagons and things."

Iona and Iva exchanged glances. While they had been feeling much the same way, yet to have those feelings exposed so plainly made them somewhat ashamed. After all Ted and Wayne were boys and just naturally liked such things.

"Don't be too hard on him, Diann. I guess this was the first time he had ever seen so many different sizes of wagons and bicycles and ball bats and footballs and everything boys like. Ted never knows when to leave such places. But it does look as if they could have seen all they needed to in nearly two hours," Iva said.

"Well, I just hope they are already home," Iona added, with a deep sigh.

"If they are not, are you going to tell the policeman?" Diann asked, her eyes wide.

"I don't know yet," Iona admitted. "Here's our bus. I don't see those boys anywhere. It's a good thing we are starting home before the crowds start."

"The crowds!" Diann exclaimed. "I'd call this a crowd."

Iva got on first. Diann was a little slow so a woman with a little boy stepped in ahead of her.

"Go on in!" Iona told Diann, giving her a push that very nearly made her miss the step.

There were not seats together so Iona crowded into the seat beside Diann, saying, "We'd better stay together."

It was not a very joyful trip home. All three of the sisters were anxious about their brothers. Finally they came to their own corner and they lost no time in leaving the bus.

"I'm going to run!" Iva called. "You can come on!"

"Let's run, too," Diann suggested, lighting out after Iva.

The girls reached the front porch one after the other, Diann leading.

"You certainly can run!" Iva admitted, panting a little.

"I run races with Wayne," Diann told her.

Into the house the girls hurried and on to the kitchen as the most likely place to find the boys. They found only Rosebud.

"What makes you all look so wild?" Rosebud asked, glancing from one to another.

"Are the boys home yet?" Iva asked.

"How come the boys would be home? Didn't they come with you all? I said for you all to stay together. Remember?" Rosebud asked, her kindly eyes snapping.

It took all three girls to explain what had happened. Rosebud stood with her hands upon her broad hips, listening, nodding her head.

"I see! I shouldn't never in the fust place let you all go off this place. It's fo'-thirty-five! Now where could boys like that be?" Rosebud asked, thoughtfully.

"Eating ice cream some place," Diann suggested.

"Like as not!" Rosebud nodded. "And how'd a policeman ever find them when there's so many places to eat ice cream?"

"Maybe they had an accident," Iona worried.

But Rosebud shook her black head. "Nobody's 'phoned to tell about ary accident. Let's see, now. O Lawd, please to he'p us to find these missin' boys. Please to keep 'em topside up and all in one piece, an' we'll sho' be full of thanks. Amen. There! We've done and got the good Lawd on our side. And that's a fact."

"Was that a prayer, Rosebud?" Diann asked.

"It sho' was, honey," Rosebud told her.

"We didn't get down on our knees," Diann reminded her.

"I was on my knees in my heart, I sho' was. The Lawd knows a prayer when He hears one no matter what position it come from. And that's a fact, too. And He's done and told me what to do. My gal Pansy's man works right near that departmental store. She knows his 'phone number. I don't. But I knows hers. I'm a-goin' to call her and tell her to 'phone Mike and tell him to look all over that store from top to bottom for two stray boys and to keep his eyes on the lookout all his way home, 'specially where ice cream's sold. If Ted and his cousin's anywheres around, Mike'll sho' find 'em!"

The call was made immediately. Presently Pansy called back to report that Mike left his work at once to try to find the missing boys. As soon as Rosebud came back to the kitchen, Iona remembered the paring knife which she gave to Rosebud. Diann whispered to Iva, "Could we have some ice cream now?"

"Rosebud, we haven't had a bite of ice cream this whole day. We planned to have some as soon as we met the boys, but when they didn't come we didn't take time to stop for any. Could we please have some now and a piece of cake?" Iva asked.

Why, certainly! And they had nice, big dishes and fat pieces of lemon jelly cake.

"The boys don't know what they're missing," Diann said, glad they hadn't stopped in town, for this was more than they would have had, maybe.

It was nearly five o'clock when Mike arrived. He found Rosebud and the girls on the front porch anxiously watching for him.

He was alone!

"I sho' didn't see Ted and his cousin nowheres atall! The clerk where the sports stuff is kept said they'd been there and he'd sold 'em a baseball. I couldn't find ary other soul that'd seen hair ner hide of 'em. I drove along slow. I didn't see 'em. Have you all told the police yet?" Mike asked.

Diann was crying.

"I wish my father was here!" she sobbed.

"Yes, and we wish our father was here, too, but he's not. Mike, do you suppose we ought to tell the police? Maybe they got lost, but Ted surely knows his way home from downtown as many times as he's been there. I just don't see what's happened," Iona said, close to tears.

"Look! Down there's the policeman on this beat. How 'bout me gettin' him to come up here and you all see what he says," Mike suggested.

"Oh, do, Mike!" Iva exclaimed.

When the officer had heard the story, he smiled reassuringly. "Give 'em time, girls! I'll call and find out if there's been any sort of accident. If not, don't report them for another hour, or so. I'll stop by along about six and see if they've come home yet. But don't worry. They likely are having a big time."

Mike went on home. Rosebud and the girls went to the kitchen to prepare dinner, for, as Rosebud said, "Like as not when they do come home, they'll be plumb starved."

Five-thirty and no boys. Since the officer had not returned, they decided there had been no accident.

Then they came! Ted and Wayne. Straight to the kitchen.

"We want water!" Ted exclaimed, going directly to the refrigerator.

"Theodore Joseph Baer! Where in the world have you been?" his sister Iva demanded.

"Wayne Maynard, why didn't you meet us as you promised to?" his sister, Diann, demanded.

Ted turned from the refrigerator, the bottle of cold water in his hand. "Why weren't you there at three o'clock?" he asked.

"We were! We waited right there at the Main Street entrance until almost four o'clock. Then we came home," Iona told him.

Ted had started to drink his water. He stopped and looked at Iona. "At the Main Street entrance?" he asked, looking rather queer.

"Yes, at the Main Street entrance where we had gone in at the beginning. Where did you come?" Iva asked. Then she added, "Did you go to the Grand Avenue entrance?"

Ted looked at Wayne. "Do you know what?" he asked, grinning. "We went to the wrong entrance. We waited, too, till three-thirty. Then we decided you'd come on home so we went back up and bought a dandy baseball. Then we got some ice cream and sandwiches. And do you know what? It took all but five cents of our money and we had to walk home! And that's a fact, Rosebud!"

"We were about to get the police after you," Diann told Wayne.

"What for?" he asked.

"How did we know what had happened to you?"

Ted looked at all of them. "Say, did we have you worried? I didn't think about that or I could have used that nickel to 'phone home to you. What makes women and girls get worried so easy?"

"Rosebud even prayed that you'd get home all right," Diann told the boys.

"And Pansy's husband, Mike, looked all over for you," Iona added.

Ted scratched his head. "I'm sorry. The next time we go out, we'll all stay together. Then if one gets lost, we'll all be lost," he decided. "How long is it till dinner? Wayne and I've had a long walk and are we hungry!"

"You ought to be," snapped Diann.

"Seems to me each an' ever' one of you all is to blame. You all promised to stay together. So if one of you all was goin' to get a whippin', the last one'd have to get it. So don't forget next time, but forget it now and take them frowns offen you all's faces. Smiles makes you all look a heap purtier. Now pitch in an' let's get this food on the table," Rosebud directed.

That night Diann knelt with Iona and Iva beside their beds and prayed. Wayne knelt with Ted in their room. When they were all cozy in bed, Diann said, "You certainly do a lot of praying. I just supposed preachers prayed in churches and when they visited people. But here you all pray. I think it's nice!"

As Iona went to sleep, she found a question disturbing her. Did Diann and Wayne know the Lord Jesus as their own Savior? She wondered.

The next morning the rain was peppering down. No one seemed in a hurry to get up. But finally the fragrance from the kitchen and Rosebud's morning hymn, "Brighten The Corner Where You Are," brought the family down the stairs.

While they were finishing their pancakes, Ted remembered. "Rosebud, did you know a circus is

THE TRIPLETS ARE SEPARATED

going to be in town tomorrow and most of next week?"

"I've been seein' 'bout it in the papers," she admitted.

"Did you ever go to a circus, Rosebud?" Iva asked.

How Rosebud's face did beam. "Why, honey, I ust to get mo' fun outen of a circus than ary other thing I ever saw, and that's a fact!" she replied, chuckling way down deep.

"Have you ever been to a circus, Wayne?" Ted asked.

Wayne shook his head. "Have you?" he asked.

"Dad took us once when we were about ten. Rosebud, do you suppose we could manage to go to this circus if the rain stops tomorrow? The parade is supposed to be at two this afternoon. Could we go to see it?" Ted wanted to know.

"Would you stay together?" Rosebud asked.

Everyone was quick to promise they would certainly stay together.

"If the rain stops, you all could go to see the parade," Rosebud decided.

The skies were watched. The clouds seemed to be breaking. And just before lunch time the sun peeped out.

"Iva, did you ask Jesus to make the sun shine?" Diann asked.

"Well, no, not exactly. The first thing this morning I asked Him to be with us through the day and help us to do just what He wanted us to do. So He must want us to go to the circus parade," Iva replied.

"I'm certainly glad. Do you know, I think Rosebud is nice," Diann admitted.

"I should say she is!" Iva agreed quickly.

8

The Triplets Have a Surprise

THE circus parade was a wonderful success. Wayne and Diann were half-afraid of the elephants, laughed and shouted at the clowns, and begged to go to the real circus.

"I'll tell you what I'm going to do!" Diann exclaimed. "I'm going to ask Jesus to help Rosebud say we may all go to the circus!"

"So'm I!" Wayne decided.

Ted, Iona, and Iva smiled.

On the way home, they talked of nothing but the parade, the animals, the bands, the riders, and the calliope.

"It would cost almost five dollars for all of us to go to the real circus," Ted reminded his cousins.

Some of the excitement vanished from their faces.

"Have we got five dollars?" Wayne asked.

"Who?" Diann wanted to know.

"All of us," Wayne replied.

"We'll have to ask Rosebud. If we didn't have to eat next week till our parents come home, we'd have five dollars," Iona replied.

The rest of the trip homeward was not quite so hilarious. Five dollars was such a lot of money! But they hurried eagerly to the kitchen and Rosebud.

"O Rosebud! It was just wonderful! But it would be more wonderful if we just have five dollars so we could go to the real circus tomorrow!" Wayne exclaimed.

"Rosebud, how hungry would we have to go if we'd use five dollars of our grocery money for the circus? We could buy a big watermelon for fifty cents and that would do for one meal, with some bread. And we could eat oatmeal for one whole day. It's real filling," Ted suggested.

"If we had to, we could live on bread and water for a day," Wayne offered, but not with much enthusiasm.

Rosebud just stood and looked at the five hopefuls before her. "Oatmeal! Watermelon! Bread an' water! Do you all want me to be fired when your parents come home? Go along and get ready fo' dinner. An' don't bother me about goin' to the circus!" she replied.

THE TRIPLETS HAVE A SURPRISE 81

But Ted took a second look at her as he left the kitchen. He heard her chuckling. "She's got something up her sleeve!" he decided.

While no one mentioned going to the circus, dinner was not as much fun as it might have been. When Wayne and Ted were alone in their room, preparing for bed, Wayne asked, "Ted, couldn't we borrow five dollars from somebody? I guess my father would help pay it back."

But Ted shook his head. No borrowing for him!

In the girls' room Diann sat upon her bed in her short blue pajamas. "Couldn't Jesus help us find five dollars somewhere so we could go to the circus?" she asked.

Iona sat down beside her. Iva sat on the floor.

"I think Jesus could do it all right if He thinks it is that important, but since we want to spend it for our own pleasure and not for anything that is really necessary, I'd hate to ask Him to perform that sort of miracle. Wouldn't you, Diann?" Iona asked.

"Yes, I guess so," she admitted, slowly. "But I do wish we could go to that circus."

"Diann, have you ever taken Jesus as your very own personal Savior?" Iona asked.

"Why, of course, I have! I was listening to a radio preacher. When he finished his sermon, he said that anyone who was listening and who wanted to be a Christian to kneel and tell Jesus all about it. So Wayne and I both knelt by our chairs and we asked Jesus to forgive all our sins and to come into our hearts. And He did! Didn't He?"

"If you meant it with all your heart, He did!" Iona told her.

"Well, we both meant it. Of course, we don't understand as well as you folks seem to, for our preacher comes only twice each month and he doesn't preach much about how to be a Christian and what to do when you are one. What should you do?" she asked. "We ought to be good. If we aren't good, I guess we're lost again."

"If you do something your parents think is disgraceful, will they say you do not belong to them, that you are not their child?" Iva asked.

"Why, no! Anyway, it wouldn't matter what they'd say, I'd still be their child because, well, just because they are my father and mother," Diann replied.

"When we accept the Lord Jesus as our very own Savior, we are born into God's great big family, we become one of His own children. We don't understand all about it because the work is done by the Holy Spirit who comes and stays with us always. So when we are born into God's family, we can't be

THE TRIPLETS HAVE A SURPRISE 83

unborn anymore than we can be unborn from our natural parents," Iva continued.

"But we have to be good," Diann said, softly.

"We are not compelled to be. If the Bible said for us to do just so many good works, we'd all try very hard to do them. But it says we are not saved by our good works because we might go around boasting about how good we are and what a lot of good we do. But when one really loves Jesus, that one will WANT to be good and do good. The Bible says we are created in Christ Jesus FOR good works, or unto good works. That means we are going to try to do good because we love Jesus. We will want to do the things that please Him. We do the things our parents will like because we love them and don't want to cause them any trouble. So when we let Jesus come into our hearts, we belong to Him and we want to please Him. See what I mean, Diann?" Iva asked.

Diann nodded her head. "Yes, but suppose someone does something wrong?"

"When you do something your mother doesn't like, what happens to you?" Iona asked.

"I get punished, if she finds it out," Diann admitted.

"Suppose she doesn't find it out right away, but you know it. Are you really happy?" Iona asked.

"No, I'm miserable. I keep wishing she'd find it out and go ahead and punish me."

"Do you know something? That's a whole lot as it is when we sin. We lose something of the joy and happiness that Jesus gives us. And we may be sure He knows all about it. He punishes us. But He doesn't ever say, 'You don't belong to Me anymore.' He says, 'Come back to Me.' And when we go back to Him, we are happy again and He forgives us and we're ready to live for Him," Iona explained.

Diann nodded her head. "I see! I guess we don't read our Bibles enough. Do you know what? I'm glad we haven't been going to lots of movies and looking at a whole lot of comic books. When we go back home, we'll know better how to live like real Christians because we have been with you."

Is it any wonder that when they prayed, they told the Lord Jesus they'd like to go to the circus, but it would be all right if they had to stay home?

Ted was the first one awake on the following morning. He wanted to see Rosebud. He remembered that chuckle!

"How come Ted's up so soon?" Rosebud asked, when he entered the kitchen.

"Oh, I woke up! Is there anything you want me to do for you, Rosebud?" Ted asked.

There was that chuckle again!

THE TRIPLETS HAVE A SURPRISE 85

"Ted, you all's the man of this here house right now. I'd like to ask you all a question."

"What is it, Rosebud?"

"Would your father be vexed if I'd let Mike drive his car this afternoon?"

Ted hesitated.

"Why doesn't he drive his own?"

Again that chuckle.

"He needs a big car to hold five passengers," Rosebud said, a broad smile brightening her face.

"Rosebud!" Ted exclaimed. "He wouldn't care. I'm sure he wouldn't!"

"Now, Ted! What you all guessin'? Lis'en here, boy, don't you all say ary word to the girls. Me'n you's goin' to have us some fun!"

"Hadn't I better get them up?" Ted asked, eagerly.

"Breakfast's mos' ready," Rosebud replied.

Ted simply bounded up the stairs and all but yanked his sisters and his cousins from their beds.

Rosebud sang heartily, "If Your Heart Keeps Right," as she finished breakfast. When Ted returned, he sang with her.

"You certainly sound happy," Diann told Ted. "So does Rosebud."

"We are happy," Ted said.

"You all pitch in now an' get your breakfast over 'cause I'm goin' to send you all on an errant right after lunch!" Rosebud announced.

Immediately appetites were not so hearty, except Ted's. He ate and ate!

"Where are we going?" Iona finally asked.

"Nowheres unless all the cleanin' up's done," Rosebud replied.

Later Iona almost bumped into Ted in the upper hall when he was hurrying to the bathroom with his clean clothes.

"Ted! You know something. What is it?" she demanded.

"You'll find out soon enough," he retorted.

When she went back to the other two girls, she reported, "Ted knows where that errand is to be. He's acting too important not to know something."

"Would Rosebud send us to the circus?" Diann asked, hopefully.

"Where would she get five dollars?" Iva asked.

Diann shrugged her shoulders. But they hurried with their work. Before noon lunch was all finished. And Mike was sitting around in the kitchen. He had backed the Baer's big car out of the garage and had cleaned the windshield.

"What is Mike doing with Dad's car?" Iva asked Ted.

"Rosebud said he wanted to use it this afternoon," was all Ted would say.

A little later, Ted called to his sisters, "Hey! Rosebud is ready for us to go on that errand!"

Not too enthusiastically the girls went into the kitchen. Mike was still there.

"Mike wants to go to the circus. Pansy can't go. She don't want him to go alone, so I'm a-sendin' all five of you all along to see he don't get lost. That's how come he's got your father's car out. Ted didn't 'spose he'd care," Rosebud began.

Hugs kept her from saying anything else.

"But Rosebud! Where did you get the five dollars? Six, with Mike's?" Diann asked.

Rosebud chuckled. Then she said, "I don't work here fo' nothin'. I gets paid. Sometimes I likes to make folks happy. I 'lowed I'd be makin' you all happy if I'd spend some o' my money an' send you all to the circus. So get goin'! An' be sho' to stay together! Mike, don't let 'em get out o' sight!"

Ted and Wayne sat in front with Mike. The girls sat in back.

"Mike's our chauffeur!" Iona exclaimed.

"We're going in style!" Diann added, sitting up very straight. "When I get home, I'm going to send Rosebud a present. I think I'll send Mike one, too!"

What a circus! No six present had more fun than this six. Mike although he was not right with his charges was where he could see them when he could take his eyes off what was going on in the ring. There was not the slightest accident anywhere and every animal did perfectly. A clown selected this group of five for many of his antics directly before them. Wayne and Diann laughed and squealed till they felt as if they couldn't laugh another little bit. Much too soon it was time to start home. Before they had time to leave their seats, Mike was right there to see that they all got out together.

When they were outside, Mike said, "Rosebud told me to buy you all some lemonade and popcorn!"

"O Mike! Really?" Diann squealed.

When Mike stopped in the driveway back home, five passengers piled out of the car from all four doors. They yelled, "Thanks, Mike! We had a wonderful time!"

Then they rushed into the kitchen.

Everyone talked at once. Diann gave Rosebud a half-empty sack, saying, "I saved some of my popcorn for you, but I couldn't bring any of my lemonade, Rosebud!"

"Thanks, honey. An' now you all listen to me. You all's got comp'ny in the livin' room, an' that's

THE TRIPLETS HAVE A SURPRISE 89

a fact. Go see who's there, but don't act so wild!" Rosebud said.

"O Rosebud, could we wash our hands in here?" Ted asked, not waiting for her reply.

"Who is it?" Iona asked.

"Is it someone grown-up, or is it someone not grown-up?" Iva asked.

"Both! Go on an' see. They'll get tired waitin'," Rosebud replied.

Ted and Wayne led the way. But as nearly as possible the five entered the room together.

"Mom!" Rosebud heard, where she was watching in the hall.

"The good Lawd bless these precious lambs an' keep 'em all in His tender Shepherd's arms!" Rosebud murmured, tears on her brown, loving face.

"And Bobby!" came Iona's happy voice.

Mother Baer and Bobby were home!